MR PATTACAKE

Stephanie Baudet

Sweet Cherry
Publishing

Published by Sweet Cherry Publishing Limited
Unit 36, Vulcan House
Vulcan Road
Leicester, LE5 3EF
United Kingdom

First published in the UK in 2017
This edition published 2020
ISBN: 978-1-78226-258-9
©Stephanie Baudet 2015
Illustrations ©Creative Books
Illustrated by Joyson Loitongbam

Mr Pattacake and the Kids' Café

Printed and bound in India
I.TP002

Pattacake, Pattacake, baker's man,
Bake me a cake as fast as you can;
Pat it and prick it and mark it with P,
Put it in the oven for you and for me.

Pattacake, Pattacake, baker's man,
Bake me a cake as fast as you can;
Roll it up, roll it up;
And throw it in a pan!

Pattacake, Pattacake, baker's man.

MR PATTACAKE
and the
KIDS' CAFÉ

'**I'VE GOT IT!**' shouted Mr Pattacake one morning, as he rushed into the kitchen waving a letter in his hand and doing the silly dance he always did when he was happy or excited. His big chef's hat **WOBBLED** like a jelly and he only just managed to catch it before it fell off altogether.

His ginger cat, Treacle, was used to these outbursts. He knew that they usually meant a cooking job for Mr Pattacake and some scraps for himself though, so he sat up and took notice.

'There's a little shop at the end of the high street,' said Mr Pattacake, puffing and flopping into a chair. 'I have rented it out and I'm going to open a café just for children.'

Treacle yawned and lay down again. It was not as interesting as he had hoped. The café part was fine because that meant food, but it was the *children* part he was not so keen on. Children did have a habit of fussing over him all the time. (Probably because he was so handsome!)

But too much attention could get annoying.

'I'm going to call it *The Kids' Café*,' said Mr Pattacake. 'Parents can leave their children there while they go shopping. The children will be able to dress up as animals and I shall make food just like the foods those animals eat. The zoo is just along the road, so I must go and study the animals' diets.'

Mr Pattacake was almost talking to himself by now, and Treacle had stopped listening and curled up for a sleep.

'I should make a list of the animal costumes and then the food I will serve.' Mr Pattacake reached for a pen and paper. Making lists was most important. It was the secret to having everything running smoothly.

Before any food could be prepared or any children enter the doors of the café, there was a lot of preparation to be done. Mr Pattacake's list of things to do looked like this:

1.   Have a sign made.

2.   Put a notice in the local paper.

3.   Buy some small tables and chairs.

4.   Decorate the café with jungle wallpaper.

5.   Buy mugs and plates and cutlery.

6.   Buy animal costumes in various sizes.

7.   Plan and print the menus.

This was going to be **fun!**

Soon everyone in the town had heard about the kids' café. Children who knew Mr Pattacake jumped up and down with excitement and couldn't wait for the café to open. Everyone had read about it in the paper and seen the colourful notice he had put in the window of the café.

A small crowd gathered when the bright yellow tables and chairs arrived and the van driver helped Mr Pattacake to carry them inside.

Once the furniture had been brought in, Mr Pattacake got ready to start decorating the café. It was very messy work, and after a couple of near misses, Treacle decided to stay safely out of the way until he was sure there was no risk of being **splattered** with wallpaper paste.

The animal costumes were a problem until Mr Pattacake met Jack, one of the little boys for whom Mr Pattacake had cooked birthday food, in the street one day. Mr Pattacake explained the problem to him.

'Why don't you use onesies?' asked Jack.

'What a great idea!' Mr Pattacake exclaimed,
'They can go on top of the children's clothes and
are easy to take on and off.'

Mr Pattacake got straight into his little yellow van and rushed off to the shop. He bought three sizes of each sort of animal onesie – giraffes, elephants, tigers, hippos, lions, penguins and chimpanzees.

Then he went to visit the zoo to find out what the animals ate.

Mr Green, the head zookeeper, thought the café was a great idea because all the interest in animals might bring more people to the zoo. He led Mr Pattacake round to see the animals and explain what they liked to eat.

The elephants were in a huge open space, and as soon as the two men arrived, one enormous grey elephant came lumbering towards them.

'This is Martha,' said Mr Green, holding out his hand to pat her trunk. 'She is an African elephant, the ones with big ears, as you see. She is a herbivore, which means that she eats all kinds of fruit and vegetables, but no meat.'

Martha reached over the fence with her trunk and plucked Mr Pattacake's big chef's hat right off his head.

'Oi!' said Mr Pattacake, trying to make a grab for it. But it was too late. Martha had tossed the hat into the air and it landed in some mud with a big squelch.

'Oh dear!' said Mr Green.

But Mr Pattacake just laughed. 'I have plenty more hats at home,' he said. 'For the elephant food, I think I shall make some delicious vegetable burgers and some fruit salad with ice cream.'

Martha twitched her big ears, she was listening to what Mr Pattacake was saying.

Next they visited the chimpanzees. There was a group of them inside a shelter. One of them came over, looked through the wire at Mr Pattacake, and then stuck out its tongue. Mr Pattacake stuck out his tongue back to the chimpanzee, who looked surprised and made a laughing sound, bouncing up and down on the ground.

'He's a mischievous one!' said the zookeeper. 'His name is Basil. He's only six months old. Chimps are like humans because they are omnivores and eat meat as well as fruit and nuts and vegetables. They also eat insects.'

'I don't think children would like eating insects,' said Mr Pattacake, 'but I can make some chocolate ones. I can also make some scrumptious nutty biscuits and cookies.'

Basil looked hard at Mr Pattacake, but didn't stick out his tongue again. He had heard what the chef had said.

They visited the tigers next. One of them was sitting in the sun and washing his enormous paw, Mr Pattacake thought he looked just like Treacle, except **MUCH** bigger!

Big cats were carnivores and only ate meat, the zookeeper explained.

'Tiger Treats,' said Mr Pattacake. 'I shall make some really tasty burgers made with the best quality meat. The children can have chips with them, too.'

The tiger's ears pricked up when it heard what Mr Pattacake said.

When they had visited the penguins and the giraffes and the crocodiles, Mr Pattacake had quite a list of food ideas for his café. The penguins had gathered round in a little group, and when Mr Pattacake mentioned the wonderful fish fingers he was going to make, they all looked at each other, and shuffled about excitedly on their little feet.

The crocodile opened its mouth wide, showing rows of big teeth and its eyes gleamed as fish cakes were mentioned.

The hippo, too, showed how wide its mouth would open, and how many cabbages it could fit in at once. Mr Pattacake suggested bubble and squeak: delicious little fried cakes made with chopped cabbage and potato, as the hippo food for his café.

The only animal food that posed a problem was the giraffe food. Giraffes just ate leaves and twigs. Whatever could he make for the café that was like that?

Mr Pattacake thanked Mr Green for all the information and went home to make a list of the food. Then he got in his little yellow van, went to buy it, and then stored it in the freezer in the café kitchen.

At last it was opening day. Mr Pattacake had decided that his Kids' Café would be open during the afternoons on school days and all day on Saturdays.

Kids' Ca

The yellow tables and chairs gleamed, the riotous wallpaper covered the walls, and in one corner there was a box containing neat piles of animal onesies.

A colourful menu was propped on each table. On them was written:

Main Courses
Delicious Elephant vegetable burgers
Tasty Tiger meaty treats and chips
Yummy Penguin fish fingers
Fabulous Crocodile fish cakes
Hearty Hippo bubble and squeak

Desserts
Elephantastic fruit salad and ice cream
Cheeky chimpanzee nutty biscuits and chocolate ants
Jolly Giraffe mint jelly leaves

Animals only drank water, which was a bit boring for children, so there were ten different kinds of juice available.

It was Saturday, and at ten o'clock Mr Pattacake unlocked the door and turned the sign to *Open*.

Treacle kept out of the way as a small crowd of children tumbled through the doorway excitedly, followed by their mums and dads. Unseen amongst all the little legs, a small tortoiseshell cat sneaked in, too. Her name was Naughty Tortie, and she hated to miss out on the possibility of some scraps. Why should Treacle get them all?

Some of the mums and dads went off shopping but one or two stayed to help Mr Pattacake in the café because it was so busy.

Halfway through the afternoon, Mr Pattacake felt so happy and excited that he did his silly dance, right there in the middle of the café. This time his big chef's hat fell off his head and everyone laughed. Seeing all the children dressed up as animals and having such a wonderful time filled Mr Pattacake with pride.

Treacle, despite his worry about being fussed over too much, was really enjoying the attention he was getting. The children fed him occasional snacks, and it was nice to be appreciated for once, too. He even let Naughty Tortie have some of the fuss, when she eventually crept out from where she'd been hiding behind the door in the toilet.

By four o'clock it had become a lot quieter and Mr Pattacake had time to sit down for five minutes (he had a bigger chair for himself because he couldn't fit into the children's chairs).

He mopped his brow with a handkerchief. **'Phew !** Weren't we busy, Treacle?' he said.

'So far my café is a great success but I hope it wasn't just because it was opening day.' Mr Pattacake looked at Naughty Tortie. 'I see you didn't want to miss out on anything either, Naughty Tortie!'

Although she was a mischievous cat, and had caused one or two mishaps, Mr Pattacake smiled at her fondly and leaned forward to stroke her.

Just then, there was a commotion outside. Mr Pattacake looked up and saw people running – all in the same direction.

Treacle and Naughty Tortie sprang up, their ears alert. All three went to the door to see what was going on.

Mr Pattacake opened the door and stepped out into the street. 'What's happening?' he asked a man who was sprinting past.

The man gabbled something and pointed at something behind him.

Traffic had come to a standstill too, and all Mr Pattacake could hear was the **pounding** of feet on the pavement and people screaming.

Then he heard something else.

It was a thundering sound, like **a lot** of feet pounding along the road. They weren't people's feet, either, because they **galloped**.

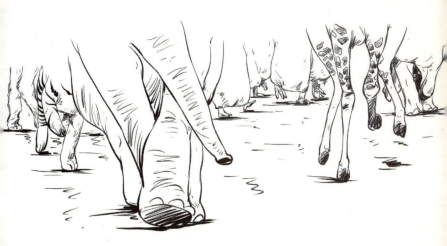

He could see something in the distance. A great jostling crowd, coming down the road.

It was a huge herd of animals!

Lots of different animals.

Leading them was a grey elephant with big ears flapping. Behind that, getting clearer as

they drew nearer, was a giraffe, its long orange and white neck high above the rest. Then came a hippo, a tiger and a chimpanzee followed by a group of penguins, waddling along.

Mr Pattacake stood bravely outside the café door (but ready to duck inside if necessary). There wasn't a single other person to be seen on the street, although there were a lot of faces at windows.

The only sound to be heard was the pounding of hooves and feet.

Mr Pattacake had a feeling that he was the reason the animals had escaped from the zoo. He recognised Martha the elephant and Basil the baby chimpanzee. Some of the others looked familiar, too.

When they saw him, the animals in front slowed down, causing those at the back to bump into them. For a moment there was a jumble of bodies struggling to get back onto their feet, accompanied by squeals, growls and grunts and Basil, the chimpanzee, laughing raucously.

Basil pushed past Mr Pattacake rudely and went into the café, causing Treacle and Naughty Tortie to leap up onto the counter in alarm. What they didn't realise was that chimpanzees were even more agile than cats. Basil hopped up on the counter beside them. They were trapped, and arched their backs, hissing at Basil, who covered

his face with his hands and whimpered in fear.
He had never seen a cat before, well, not ones as
small as this!

The crocodile pushed past Mr Pattacake
too, and so did a group of penguins. Martha,
the elephant, couldn't get through the café door
although she tried.

She just waved her trunk around, sniffing. Then she snatched Mr Pattacake's big chef's hat right off his head, just as she had done when he visited the zoo.

But before she could toss it in the air, Basil, the baby chimp, dashed out of the café and swung onto Martha's back, snatching the big chef's hat as he went. Then he tried to put it on his head, but it was far too big. The hat went right over Basil, making him shriek with fear.

For a moment he struggled inside the hat before finally pulling it off and throwing it in the air. Mr Pattacake lunged forward and caught it, then put it firmly back on his head.

Mr Pattacake stood surrounded by animals, and he quickly realised that he was in danger of being squashed as more and more of them tried to get into the café.

Then all of the animals started talking at once. Or at least roaring and chattering and snorting and doing whatever elephants do.

The tiger came and stood in front of Mr Pattacake, looked him in the eye, and roared softly.

'I don't understand,' said Mr Pattacake, his voice shaking, as well as his big chef's hat. After all, this was a wild tiger, which could attack him at any moment.

It had **MUCH** bigger teeth than Treacle, and no doubt **MUCH** bigger claws, too.

Then an idea popped into his mind.

Mr Pattacake looked behind him into the café, to where Treacle and Naughty Tortie were huddled next to the microwave oven. Treacle was staring intently at the tiger.

Now, Mr Pattacake had been around cats for a long time and he could read their minds. Certainly, he could read Treacle's.

And as Treacle was a cat, just as a tiger was, he could read the tiger's mind. So Mr Pattacake was getting a translation of what the tiger was saying.

'We heard what Mr Pattacake said when he came to visit the zoo,' said the tiger. 'He was going to open a café for children where they could dress up to look like us animals and eat what we eat. Except that the food Mr Pattacake described sounded **MUCH** better than what we have, so we decided to escape from our home at the zoo, and come and taste Mr Pattacake's food.'

'My goodness!' said Mr Pattacake. 'I haven't got enough food for you all! There isn't room in the café, either, and many of you would break the little chairs if you sat on them!'

He stood and thought for a moment while the tiger and all the animals shuffled about restlessly.

Basil, the chimpanzee, who had gone back into the café, ran out holding a banana in one hand and a nutty biscuit in the other.

The animals surged forward and Mr Pattacake held up his hands and shouted '**STOP!**' so loudly that they stopped in surprise.

Then there was another sound. The keepers from the zoo had arrived.

'Are you all right, Mr Pattacake?' shouted Mr Green, the head keeper, who had shown Mr Pattacake around the zoo.

'Yes, thank you,' Mr Pattacake shouted back.

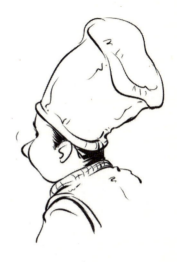

'I don't know what's got into them,' said Mr Green. 'Just as the keepers were about to close the pens for the night, the animals surged out, knocking the keepers over. I was just closing the main gates, when Martha rammed into them. There was nothing I could do.' He shook his head in amazement. 'They must have planned it. It's most unusual for different species to communicate like that!'

The keepers began to try to herd the animals away from the café and back towards the zoo, but they all refused, and stood firmly where they were.

The crocodile snapped at the keepers' feet if they came too close, and the tiger growled.

'Oh dear, I don't know what we can do,' said Mr Green. 'We'll have to get the police and the army to help, but that will take time.'

'I know a better way,' said Mr Pattacake, smiling. 'You see, I know why they have come. My cat, Treacle, can understand the tiger, and I can understand Treacle. It seems that when I came to visit your zoo, the animals heard my plans for food for the children's café, and they decided that they wanted to come and taste it for themselves. They think it sounds better than their food at the zoo.'

Mr Green nodded. 'I see,' he said. 'But you can't possibly have enough for them all.'

'I have some leftovers from today,' said Mr Pattacake. 'A few of the animals can taste them, but I have an even better idea.' He looked at the tiger, and spoke loudly so that Treacle could hear, and translate.

'My idea is that once a week, on a Sunday, I arrange a little party at the zoo. The first week will be for the tigers, the second week for the elephants, and so on, so that each group of animals has a little party every now and again.'

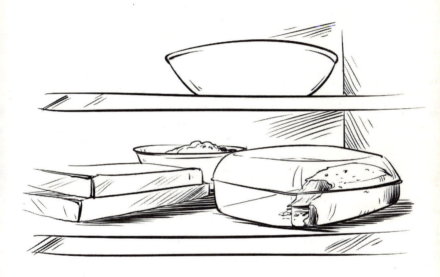

The tiger looked at Treacle, who meowed the message, which soon spread to all the animals.

One or two began backing away from the café so that Mr Pattacake could get inside to fetch the leftovers.

He gave some *Tasty Tiger Meaty Treats* to the tiger (without the chips).

He held out some *Delicious Elephant Vegetable Burgers* to Martha the elephant, who grabbed them with her trunk and stuffed them into her mouth.

The penguins shared the *Yummy Penguin Fish Fingers.*

Some *Fabulous Crocodile Fish Cakes* were given to the crocodiles.

The *Hearty Hippo Bubble and Squeak* was given to the hippos.

The chimpanzees crowded round for some *Nutty Biscuits* and *Chocolate Ants,* but they didn't like the chocolate ants and spat them out. They preferred real ones.

The only animals that were not happy were the giraffes. *Giraffe Mint Jelly Leaves* were not to their taste, so they wandered off down the road to find some *real* leaves in someone's garden.

Mr Pattacake would have to think of something special for *their* party.

Meanwhile, those who had been given some food chewed while all the others watched.

Mr Pattacake almost held his breath. What if, after all this, the animals didn't like the food? Would they be angry? Would they stampede his café and run rampage up the street?

He tried to back away a little, nearer to where the zookeepers were standing.

There was silence.

Then, one after another, the animals showed their pleasure at the food. The tiger licked his lips over and over, the elephant reached inside the café again with her trunk, looking for more. The crocodile had a pleasant gleam in its eye and the penguins nodded their heads and stamped their little feet in agreement.

Soon they began to turn around and walk back up the road towards the zoo, and the keepers hardly had to do anything but follow.

But before they had gone far, however, there was a whirring droning noise, and the calm animals began to skitter about restlessly, jostling each other. Some looked as though they were going to break away and stampede.

Mr Pattacake knew that would be a disaster. He shaded his eyes and looked towards where the noise was coming from.

A helicopter! It must be the police or the army.

He ran towards the sound, waving his big chef's hat in the air. He must get them to turn around before they spooked the animals.

He looked up in the air and saw that the people in the helicopter had seen him too. He gestured for them to turn around and go back.

A soldier was leaning out of the open door. 'We believe that the animals have escaped from the zoo. Do you need any help?' he shouted.

'No, thank you,' Mr Pattacake shouted back. 'It's all under control.'

The man waved and the helicopter turned around and zoomed away.

Mr Pattacake mopped the sweat off his forehead with a paper serviette, before replacing his big chef's hat on his head. He didn't even have the energy to do his silly dance.

The animals had settled again and were making their way calmly back to the zoo.

Gradually, curious people ventured back into the high street, anxious to know what the fuss was all about.

Mr Pattacake stared at the chaos inside his café. The tables and chairs were all in a jumbled heap, although only one chair appeared to be broken. It was in tiny pieces as if the hippo had sat on it.

There was mud on the floor, and other things too, which made Mr Pattacake wrinkle up his nose. He had a lot of cleaning up to do before he opened again on Monday.

What exciting stories he would be able to tell the children though!

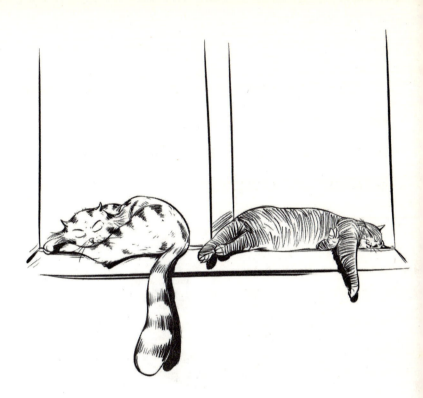

Treacle and Naughty Tortie lay on the windowsill in a patch of sunshine. Treacle was very tired after all the translating he had done between Mr Pattacake and the tiger. After all, although a tiger is a cat, it's a different kind of cat, and its language is different from that of a pet cat. Treacle thought he had done very well and deserved a rest.

Naughty Tortie, too, had had an exciting day, as well as sharing the scraps with Treacle. She decided that maybe she wouldn't be so mischievous in future.

By opening time the following Monday afternoon, Mr Pattacake had the café looking spick and span again. This time, there was an even bigger number of children waiting outside, although some of their parents looked a little bit worried.

Mr Pattacake opened the door.

'Don't worry,' he said. 'The animals will not be escaping from the zoo today. I have promised to throw a party for them every week on Sundays. You can see them enjoying their parties at the zoo if you want, and they'll be safely behind a fence.'

By the end of the afternoon, Mr Pattacake had begun thinking about what he was going to make for the animal's parties. First he was going to cook for the tigers...

As the door closed on the last customer, Mr Pattacake turned the sign to 'CLOSED' and sat down at the counter to make a list.